Over in Australia
Amazing Animals Down Under

By Marianne Berkes
Illustrated by Jill Dubin

Dawn Publications

Over in Australia
In a swamp in the sun
Lived a fierce crocodile
And her little *hatchling* one.

"Snap," said the mother.
"I snap," said the one.
So they snipped and they snapped
In a swamp in the sun.

Over in Australia
Looking like a kangaroo
Lived a smaller wallaby
And her little *joeys* **two**.

"Hop," said the mother.
"We hop," said the **two**.
So they hopped, then they stopped,
Looking like a kangaroo.

Over in Australia
In a eucalyptus tree
Lived a cuddly gray koala
And her little *joeys* three.

"Munch," said the mother.
"We munch," said the three.
So they munched and they crunched
In a eucalyptus tree.

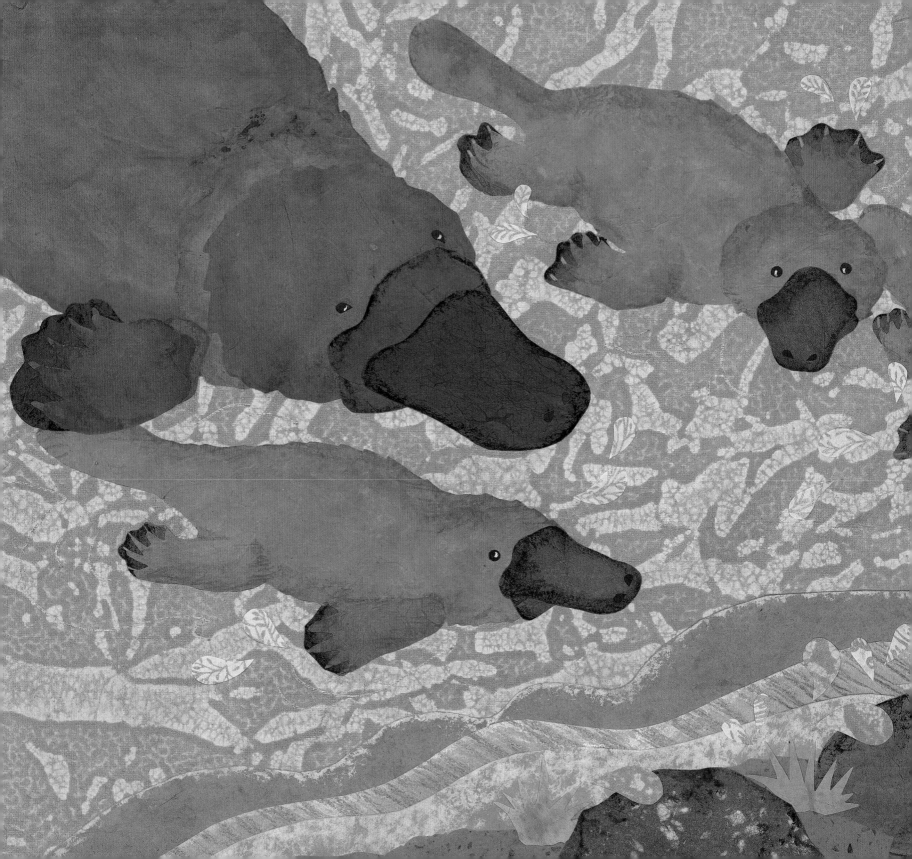

Over in Australia
Where they swam to the shore
Lived a sleek platypus
And her *platypups* four.

"Splash," said the mother.
"We splash," said the four.
So they splished and they splashed
As they swam to the shore.

Over in Australia
Where the wild flowers thrive
Lived a rainbow lorikeet
And her little *chicks* **five**.

"Chit," said the mother.
"We chit," said the five.
So they chitted and they chattered
Where the wild flowers thrive.

Over in Australia
Where the tall grasses mix
Lived a short stocky wombat
And her little *joeys* **six**.

"Dig," said the mother.
"We dig," said the **six**.
So they dug deep in dirt
Where the tall grasses mix.

6

Over in Australia
In a tree that reached to heaven
Lived a furry sugar glider
And her little *joeys* seven.

"Lap," said the mother.
"We lap," said the seven.
So they lapped on the sap
In a tree that reached to heaven.

Over in Australia
Where she bowed to her mate
Lived a tall friendly brolga
And her little *chicks* **eight**.

"Dance," said the mother.
"We dance," said the **eight**.
So they danced and they pranced
As she bowed to her mate.

Over in Australia
In a sandy place to dine
Lived a hungry, long-eared bilby
And her little *joeys* **nine**.

"Slurp," said the mother.
"We slurp," said the **nine**.
So they slurped and they burped
In a sandy place to dine.

Over in Australia
Acting like a mother hen
Lived a huge father emu
And his little *chicks* ten.

"Zig," said the father.
"We zig," said the ten.
So they zigged and they zagged
With their father "mother hen."

10

All around Australia
Where most species are unique,
While the parents all are resting,
Their kids play hide and seek.

"Find us," say the children,
"From ten to one."
When you find all the children
This rhyme isn't done.

Go back and start over
And spy with your eyes
To find a hidden creature—
Every page has a surprise!

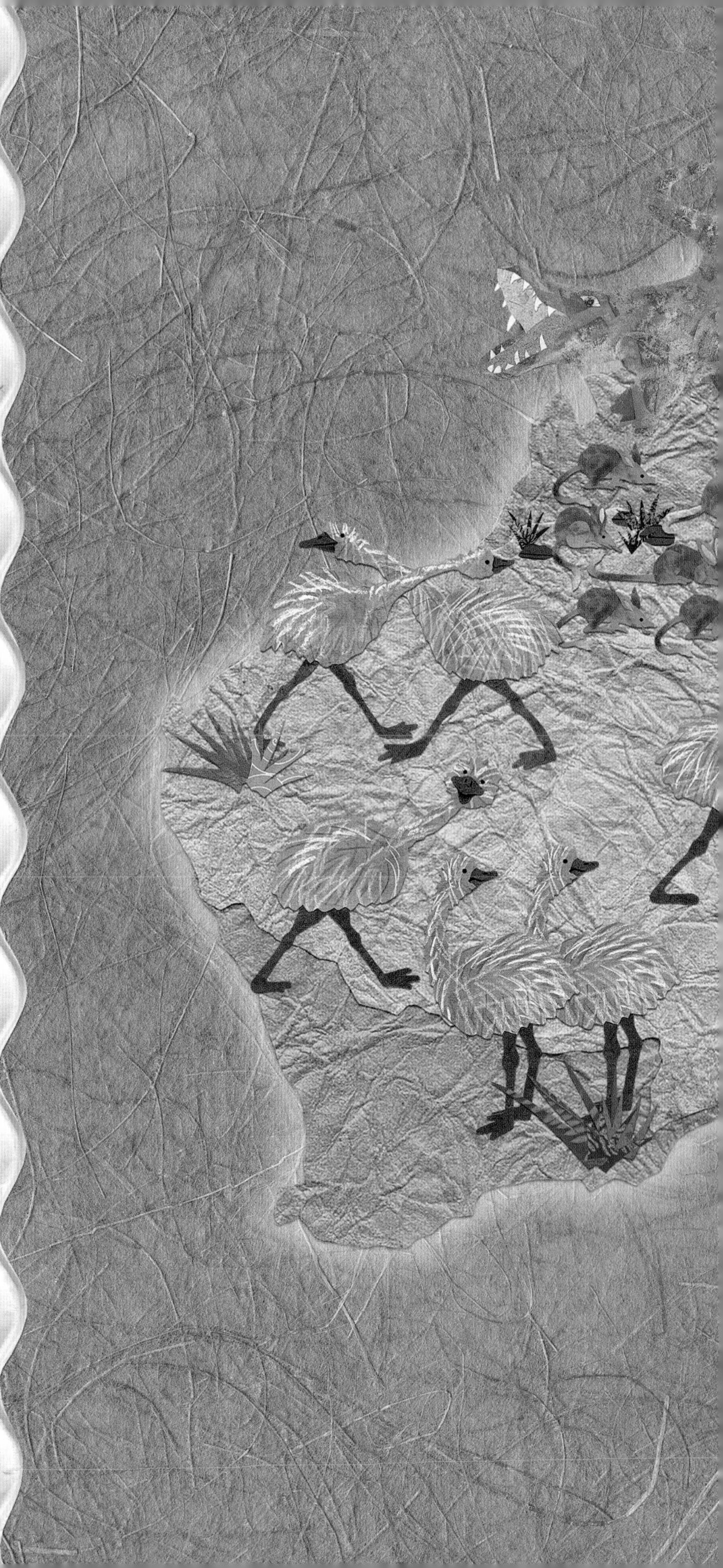

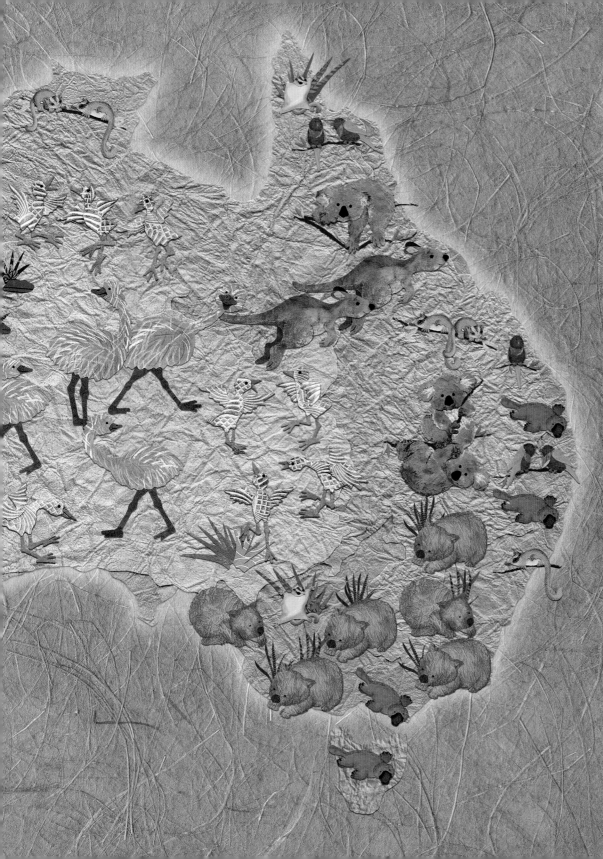

Find Us!

- 10   Emus
- 9   Bilbies
- 8   Brolgas
- 7   Sugar Gliders
- 6   Wombats
- 5   Lorikeets
- 4   Platypuses
- 3   Koalas
- 2   Wallabies
- 1   Crocodile

 Desert

 Grassland

 Forest

Fact or Fiction?

The animals in this story behave as they have been portrayed—crocodiles *snap*, koalas *munch*, and platypuses *splash*. That's a fact! It is also a fact that many of them live only in Australia.

But do they have the number of babies as in this rhyme? No, that is fiction! Do the babies live where they are shown on the map of Australia? Approximately.

Baby animals are cared for in very different ways, depending upon the species. Marsupials, like koalas and wallabies, give birth to partially-formed babies that develop in the mother's pouch until they are ready to feed on their own. A mother crocodile carries her hatchlings to the water's edge and stays nearby to protect them until they wander off to fend for themselves. After a mother emu lays eggs, the father emu incubates them and cares for them after they hatch. Baby lorikeets, though, are cared for by both the mother and father. Nature has very different ways of ensuring the survival of species.

Australian Animals Are Amazing!

Although Australia is called a continent because it's so big, it is also an island, surrounded by vast areas of ocean. Because of its isolation, some animals established themselves there and nowhere else. In other words, they are *endemic*, or native to the country. Australia is unique in that around 80 percent of its animals are endemic. They live in Australia's primary ecosystems: deserts, forests and grasslands.

Many Australian mammals are *marsupials* (mahr-SOUP-ee-uhls), a special kind of mammal in which the mothers give birth to their young and then carry their babies in a pouch until they are able to survive on their own. The best known marsupials are kangaroos. There are 46 different kangaroo species in Australia. Koalas and wombats are also familiar marsupials. Only a few marsupial species are found outside of Australia, one of them being the opossum.

Marsupials aren't the only unusual mammals in Australia. There are also *mammals that lay eggs*! These are called *monotremes*. Two such animals that live in Australia are the platypus and echidna.

Australia also has the greatest number of reptiles of any country—917 species. Reptiles mentioned in this book include the crocodile, gecko, lizard, and python.

The "Hidden" Australian Animals

The FRILLED NECK LIZARD is a species in the Dragon lizard family. The frill around its neck expands like an umbrella when the lizard is frightened. When it rests, the frill folds around its shoulders. It hunts in trees and on the ground for insects, spiders and smaller reptiles.

DINGOES are related to dogs and wolves. Adults are about the size of a medium dog. They have a keen sense of smell, and hunt at night. They eat rats, kangaroos, rabbits, and other animals, swallowing the meat in large chunks. Dingoes do not bark, but sometimes they howl.

The KOOKABURRA is the largest bird in the kingfisher family. A common and familiar bird in Australia, the kookaburra is well known for its loud call which sounds like human laughter. Kookaburras live in family groups and usually nest in a hole in a tree.

The ECHIDNA (ih-KID-nuh), like the platypus, is a shy and unusual egg-laying mammal. Unlike the platypus, it does not swim in water but searches for food on land, making a sniffing noise as it goes. It has sharp spines and a tube-like snout. It is also called a "spiny anteater" because its long sticky tongue catches termites and ants.

COCKATOOS are members of the parrot family. The Sulphur-Crested Cockatoo (illustrated) is one of Australia's best known parrots with its large, yellow head crest. Cockatoos feed on seeds, berries, nuts and leaf buds.

The TIGER QUOLL is a carnivorous marsupial that looks like a cross between a cat and an opossum, with a pointed snout and long tail. Its red-brown fur is covered with white spots of various sizes. Once very common, their numbers have greatly declined.

The BLACK SWAN is a large graceful water bird that breeds mainly in wetlands. Its body is mostly black with a red beak tipped in white. The black swan reaches under water with its long neck to eat water plants, including the roots.

The BARKING GECKO got its name because it makes a barking sound as a defense. They are orange-brown, with small spots arranged in bands across their bodies. They are active at night and eat mainly insects and spiders.

The WOMA PYTHON is a very large snake that wraps itself around its prey, squeezes it to death, and swallows it whole. They live in arid and semi-arid environments.

RINGTAIL POSSUMS are active at night, eating flowers, fruit, and leaves from the trees in which they live. The joeys crawl into the mother's pouch after they are born and drink milk for about two months. Then they ride on the mother's or father's back until they fully mature.

About the Animals

SALTWATER CROCODILES are the world's largest reptile, with males sometimes 20 feet long. They can travel far out to sea, but usually live in the rivers and swamps in the north of Australia. Saltwater crocs have long, robust snouts and strong jaws that *snap* up animals both small and large which they swallow in large chunks. Crocs like to bask in the sun. When they go back to lie in swamp water, they can hardly be seen because their eyes and nostrils are on the top of their heads. The mother protects her nest while the eggs are incubating. Then she carries the **hatchlings** to the water's edge and stays nearby until they leave and fend for themselves.

WALLABIES belong to the family *Macropodidae* (ma-crow-POD-uh-dee) which means "big feet." They use their powerful hind legs to *hop* at high speeds and jump great distances. Their large tails help them to stop and prop themselves up when sitting. A baby wallaby, like its larger relative the kangaroo, is called a **joey**, and lives in the mother's pouch until it develops enough to survive on its own. Wallabies are *herbivores* (plant-eaters) that eat mostly grasses and plants.

KOALAS look like cuddly teddy bears, but are actually *marsupials*. The **joeys** live in their mother's pouch for about six months. After that the young koala is carried on its mother's back until it is quite large. Koalas spend their days resting and sleeping high above the ground in forests of eucalyptus trees. They *munch* on leaves of eucalyptus trees, absorbing enough moisture from the leaves so they do not need to drink. Like their close relatives, the wombats, koalas have a pouch which faces backwards, which would seem like a disadvantage since they climb trees, but the joeys do not fall out.

The **PLATYPUS** (PLAT-ah-puss) is an unusual *monotreme* mammal with characteristics of both a mammal and a bird. It has sleek, waterproof fur and a furry, flat tail like some mammals, but also a bill and webbed feet somewhat like a duck. Platypuses lay eggs and after the eggs hatch the mothers nurse their babies. They live in burrows near a riverbank. The platypus is a *carnivore*, or meat eater, and uses its sensitive bill to find its prey—worms, snails and shrimp—in the mud. Its webbed feet and flat tail help it *splash* as it swims.

RAINBOW LORIKEETS are medium-sized Australian parrots with brightly colored feathers. Lorikeets eat flowers, pollen, nectar, seeds, insects, and some fruit, often while hanging upside-down from branches. They have a curved red bill and a brush-tipped tongue. Lorikeets *chit* and *chatter* as they fly. They usually mate for life. The female lays two or three eggs in a tree cavity high above the ground and incubates them for about 25 days while the male feeds her. Both parents then feed the **chicks**.

WOMBATS live in long underground burrows and have flat, wide paws with long, curved claws. As marsupials, their pouch is distinctive. Its opening faces the mother's back legs, which prevents dirt from covering the baby while the mother is *digging* deep in dirt. The **joey** will stay in the pouch until it can walk on its own. Short and stocky, wombats shuffle as they walk and are *nocturnal*, or active at night. Wombats are *herbivores*, or plant-eaters, eating mostly grasses, leaves and roots.

SUGAR GLIDERS like sweet food, as you might guess from the name. They are small tree-dwelling marsupials with fox-like ears and big eyes. Sugar gliders rest in nests in hollow trees during the day. They have two thin flaps of skin that span from the fifth finger to the first toe on each side of the body. This allows them to glide over 165 feet through the air from tree to tree at night and *lap* up sap, nectar and pollen. A tail as long as the rest of their body helps them steer as they "fly." The female has a pouch in which her **joeys** develop and nurse.

BROLGAS are tall cranes that live primarily in wetlands. They are well known for their mating dance, which begins with the crane picking up some grass, tossing it into the air, and catching it in its bill. The brolga then leaps into the air with its wings outstretched—bowing, jumping, and prancing about with its partner. As they *dance* together they often make loud trumpeting calls. Both parents incubate the eggs and guard the **chicks** for up to a year. Brolgas are *omnivores*—they eat both plants and animals.

The BILBY is a species of desert bandicoot. It is a favorite Australian marsupial that is sometimes called a "pinkie" because of its long pink nose and big rabbit-like ears. It lives in deserts in an underground den which it digs with its strong, clawed feet. An *omnivore*, it detects insects, lizards, mice, some fungi, grass seeds, and fruit with its pointed nose and slurps them up with its tongue. It swallows a large amount of sand with its food. When a bilby has a **joey**, it stays in her pouch for about eighty days. Bilbies are now endangered and no longer common in Australia, so chocolate Easter bilbies have taken the place of the Easter bunny. Sales have raised thousands of dollars to help protect this unique creature.

The EMU is the world's second largest bird after the ostrich. Emus can't fly, but they can run very fast—over 30 miles per hour. When chased by a predator, like an eagle from the sky, the emu will run in a *zig-zag* pattern with its long powerful legs to avoid being caught. Each foot has three forward facing toes but no hind toe. Emus are great swimmers and often play in water or mud. However, these days in Australia they are most commonly found in desert areas. This huge bird lives in flocks and primarily eats grass, seeds, flowers, fruit, and some insects. The female lays up to 20 eggs, which the male incubates for about eight weeks, never leaving the nest. When the eggs hatch, the father looks after the **chicks** for another six months.

Tips from the Author

This book offers many opportunities for activities. Here are some ideas.

DRAMATIC PLAY—Sing and act out what each animal does: *snap*, *hop*, *splash*, and so on. Kids can also make masks of the animals. See: http://www. enchantedlearning.com/ crafts/Mask.shtml

CUT-OUTS AND STICK PUPPETS—Using printouts from http://www.enchantedlearning.com/ coloring/Australia.shtml, color and cut out each animal and glue onto tongue depressors for stick puppets. Or place them on a flannel board as you read or sing the story. Older students can place their cut-outs on a map of Australia, in the appropriate biome.

WHO AM I?—Write two sentences describing an animal in this book, not mentioning which one it is. For example, *I am a small marsupial that glides from tree to tree. I love to lap up sweet sap.*

SNIP-SNAP CROCODILES—Draw a crocodile or enlarge the baby croc in this book, tracing it onto a recycled file folder. Cut it out in three separate pieces: Upper jaw, lower jaw with body, and tail. Kids can color scales, a red tongue, and glue on a google eye. Stick brass paper fasteners through the tail and the upper jaw attaching them to the body. Or make a clothespin alligator that "snaps." See: www.busybeekidscrafts.com/ Clothes-Pin-Alligator.html

A VENN DIAGRAM—Choose two marsupials in this book and compare them in a venn diagram. http://www.graphic.org/venbas.html

WRITE A DIAMANTE POEM—A diamante poem is a poem in the shape of a diamond. Compare an animal in the story with the hidden animal on the same page. See www.readwritethink.org/files/resources/interactives/ diamante/ to get started.

Discuss

- Use an *action* verb for each "hidden" animal to show how it might behave. (e.g. a kookaburra "laughs").
- What were the ten featured animals called as babies? How many have the same "baby" name?

- Which Australian animals are *herbivores*? Which ones are *carnivores*? Are there any *omnivores*?
- How many mammals in this book are *marsupials*? Which animal in the main story is a *monotreme*? Name another one among the hidden animals.
- Animals that live in Australia's Great Barrier Reef were not a part of the story. Go onto http://www.reef.crc.org.au/discover/ plantsanimals/facts_plantanimal.htm and pick an animal that you could substitute in this story.

DO FURTHER RESEARCH—The map on the last page shows approximately where the animals live. Ask children to learn more exactly the range of each animal.

BOOKMARKS—Click on the "Teaching Tools" button at www.dawnpub. com to download reproducible bookmarks for this book.

Discover more in books . . .

A Field Guild of the Mammals of Australia, P. Menthorst & F. Knight (Oxford University Press, 2005)

Alligators and Crocodiles, Trudi Strain Trueit (Children's Press, 2003)

Birds of Australia, Ken Simpson (Princeton University Press, 2004)

Pocket Babies and Other Amazing Marsupials, Sneed B. Collard III (Darby Creek, 2007)

. . . and on the internet

Parks Australia: http://www.environment.gov.au/parks/

Australia Museum: http://www.austmus.gov.au/factsheets/index.htm

Australia Zoo: http://www.australiazoo.com.au/

Photos of animals: http://www.ozanimals.com

Unique Australian animals: http://australian-animals.net/

I would love to hear from educators and parents with creative ways to use this book. My web site is www.marianneberkes.com.

Tips from the Illustrator

The illustrations in this book are collages. Collages can be made from a variety of materials glued together to create a picture. I've used paper, combining colors and textures to create the illustrations. After careful research of each animal and their environment, I select paper that best shows the animal's fur, feathers or skin. While I maintain the reality of each animal and their environment, I also keep in mind my own ideas of color and design. I may choose a paper for the pattern or texture that wouldn't be found in nature. You can see this in the night sky of the sugar gliders and the pattern on the leaves of the lorikeets.

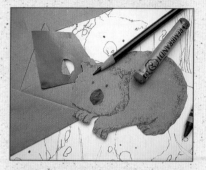

I make a detailed drawing of each illustration. Using a copy of my drawing as a pattern, I cut each piece out of decorative paper. Sometimes I use a toothpick to glue down small pieces. I spread a very thin layer of glue to assemble the elements. It really doesn't take much glue. I put the whole thing between two pieces of acetate and press it under the heaviest books I have. This assures that each finished piece will lie flat. It's like putting a puzzle together! Each animal is made up of a variety of glued-together shapes. All the animals are glued to the background. I finish with colored pencils and pastels to add details, shading, and emphasis.

You can create your own animal collages of Australian animals, or animals in your neighborhood, or your own pet. Also flowers are good subjects for collages, such as the flannel flower from Australia that I used as background around the text. Look around you and collect paper that appeals to you. You can use strips from a brown paper bag to make long grass like the wallabies are hopping through. Another part of the bag can be cut out for fur, such as that of the wombat. Try using a crayon, colored pencil, pastel or chalk to make shading on the body and details like spots, stripes and faces. Crinkled crepe paper or colored tissue paper would make great water, like for the splashing platypus. See how the brolgas are wading through cellophane water with sandpaper as their beach. You can find patterns using newspapers, old magazines, wrapping paper or greeting cards. Look for details within the designs that you find interesting. Use your imagination, make it your own—and have fun.

Also by Marianne Berkes

Over in the Ocean: In a Coral Reef, illustrated by Jeanette Canyon — With unique and outstanding style, this book portrays the vivid community of creatures that inhabit the ocean's coral reefs. Its many awards include the National Parenting Publications Gold Award.

Over in the Jungle: A Rainforest Rhyme, illustrated by Jeanette Canyon — As with "Ocean," this book captures a rainforest teeming with remarkable creatures, and was named an "Outstanding Product" by iParenting Media for 2007.

Over in the Arctic: Where the Cold Winds Blow, illustrated by Jill Dubin — Another charming counting rhyme introducing creatures of the tundra, illustrated with cut paper art. Honored with a Mom's Choice Gold Award.

Seashells by the Seashore, illustrated by Robert Noreika — Kids discover, identify, and count twelve beautiful shells to give Grandma for her birthday.

Going Around the Sun: Some Planetary Fun, illustrated by Janeen Mason — Our Earth is part of a fascinating planetary family: eight planets and an odd bunch of solar system "cousins." Here young ones can get a glimpse of our remarkable neighborhood, and our place in a very big universe.

Going Home: The Mystery of Animal Migration, illustrated by Jennifer DiRubbio — Many animals migrate "home," often over great distances. This winning combination of verse, factual language, and beautiful illustrations is a solid introduction.

Some Other Nature Awareness Books from Dawn Publications

Around One Log: Chipmunks, Spiders, and Creepy Insiders — Years after a great oak tree tumbled to the ground, a whole community of animals—salamanders, roly-polies, chipmunks, and many more—made it their home. Is the old tree now dead? Or alive? This is the latest in a series by Anthony Fredericks that also includes *Under One Rock*, *Near One Cattail*, *In One Tidepool*, *Around One Cactus*, and *On One Flower*.

In the Trees, Honeybees — a remarkable inside-the-hive view of a wild colony of honeybees, along with simple rhymes and solid information, make this a favorite among bee-lovers.

THE BLUES GO BIRDING series features a unique team of bluebirds who are crazy about bird-watching! Their delightful antics will introduce a new generation to the wonderful sport of birding. In *The BLUES Go Birding Across America* they visit iconic American birds including the eagle, woodpecker, robin, meadowlark, and others. In *The BLUES Go Birding at Wild America's Shores* they visit shorebirds on every coast. In *The BLUES Go Extreme Birding* they see record-breaking birds worldwide such as fastest-diving, highest-flying, and deepest diving.

Dawn Publications is dedicated to inspiring in children a deeper understanding and appreciation for all life on Earth. You can browse through our titles, download resources for teachers, and order at www.dawnpub.com, or call 800-545-7475.